My Life:

The Last Photo

Author: Denzel Walker

Started: August 4, 2008   Finished: January 11, 2009

Order this book online at www.trafford.com
or email orders@trafford.com

Most Trafford titles are also available at major online book retailers.

Printed in the United States of America.

ISBN: 978-1-4269-4288-4 (sc)
ISBN: 978-1-4269-4289-1 (ebk)

*Our mission is to efficiently provide the world's finest, most comprehensive book publishing
service, enabling every author to experience success. To find out how to publish your book,
your way, and have it available worldwide, visit us online at www.trafford.com*

Trafford rev. 09/08/2010

 www.trafford.com

North America & international
toll-free: 1 888 232 4444 (USA & Canada)
phone: 250 383 6864 ♦ fax: 812 355 4082

Table Of Contents

Chapter (001): Chapter Zero

"Hey did you know there is about… uhh, ok forget percentages. Anyway a lot of people, meaning children, get picked on and still do today, but that didn't happen to everyone though. Ya see, I met this boy when I was really really young, and his personality is remarkably unique. He's so different, that most of the kids at school picked on him. Sometimes even I would, but I would always protect him, eventually…

Then something bad happened, that even all the kids looked in fear. As I looked at him with a gaze… down his neck blood poured from the victim to the face of his permanently angered face… he practically put a death scar on everyone's forehead… blank… a blank feeling… A foreboding in everyone's eyes plunged everywhere. He dropped the victim to the ground, and then suddenly looking frightened as if he had woke from a daze, calling me, with tears brawling from his eyes, calling me again. I rushed over to him like wind, embraced him, and sat as every one covered the area with woe. The police came, and blamed it on some girl instead, but everyone had this sight, this thought, slashed in their hearts. Soon after everyone forgot about it and went on, they never insulted him ever again. Kind of ignoring him, so he stuck by me and looked up to me, because I was the only one who sincerely liked him. Every morning when I come to see him, I try to forget this… omen. Still I took a picture so I could-… My name is *Ami Naming* of team 001 telling my-… our story."

"As where Ami left off, my name is *Zuman Claw* of team 001 and yes… some things are better left unsaid sometimes. Anyway, before I give away anything away… let's start back to…when they were both teens, and trust me, this is the time you want to start at." "Because a full life is sometimes…" (Simultaneously) "… Thought between a photo!"

Chapter (001):

A New Beginning

Ami was just talking to her friends recently. Usually she's constantly thinking about… "Him," but friends seem to have come her way though.

"So I'll see you tomorrow at 1:30 ok Ami," said girl number one.

"…" Ami paused to herself.

"Hey Ami you ok?"

"Yeah you seem, a little sad," said girl number two.

"… Huh, yeah sure… just thinking about something."

"Well anyway, we'll see you tomorrow, kay Ami… bye."

"…Bye."

As Ami watched her friends leave, she quickly turned around and continued walking into the grassed field blooming with trees and daffodils. While looking at her on designs...

"I finally have the designs for-

WHOOOSSHHH!!!

"Whoa!" Ami yelled, as something vrooshed by while putting back her designs. She happens to look back at "it" to see that it was just the same amount of speed power she saw when she was little…

"… My old friend, is finally back," Ami said as she leaned against a tree prominently and confidently surprised. Ami grabbed held of the ground like stretching out hair beneath her feet, like grass. She took a track starters position and forcefully plunged herself forward the same speed as "it," and then cutting it off from its destination, catching up to it to only find out that the "it," Ami was referring to, was long gone...

She lost her track of thought, and then had a flashback

"Hey what are you doing on the ground, need some help?"
"Yeah, thanks… what's your name?"
"Hehehe, Ha! My name is Ami Naming. So question boy, what's yours?"

She was startled but gained conscious soon after… weird

She then looked up in a surprise and a gaze to notice something. "Huh… Hyki is it really you…?"Ami said with a tear in her eye. "… Ami?"

Both Ami and Hyki were both exited to see each other after so long. It explains why Ami is so mopy most of the time. After the incident when they were children, an incident that drove everything out of its path, they're finally back, to be whole again. As they both stood, they would pause to look at the others every detail. A streak of importance struck the air, like a flower blooming at speeds of 10 buffalo running down hill. Rushing to each other, they both ran as their smiles turned to pure heart, embracing each other. Ami smiled with tears of joy, while Hyki tried not to cry, but instead said…

"Ami… Ami… you came back…" startled in his tears almost screaming.

"Back to me…" Hyki blurted out.

A shock-like chill spun up Ami's spine, like a tornado turning into a hurricane, and into that, she said…

"I-I… I miss you too!"

When letting go of each other, Ami leaned against a tree, relaxed, while Hyki plopped to the ground exhausted. Ami seemed to notice, then realize, that Hyki was wearing a new outfit: A mechanical thought tail, and upgraded Pole, new hair style, and a book of thoughts she presumed.

"What's with the new stuff?" Ami said.

"Well, it kinda started, or erupted, from that fight you remember. Ever since I gave you some of my inner strength… now I need new parts, more thoughts, and a different look… so I can start over again."

"Hello, my name is *Hyki Momoshe* of team 001… It's kinda funny what I've been going through, all of my life troubles, till today, but with all of my friends to help me along the way, I gave others encouragement too. Recently Ami has talked about me, and Zuman too, but... after a while you just gotta say to yourself... why me? I mean I could understand from any other person's perspective, but still I wonder...... some things I just want to get rid of, regardless of what happens to me. And some, I wanna get back... signing off until next time, eh?"

"So do you want to go to my house, I built it on my own ya know?" Hyki said with a grin on his face.

"Uh sure, why not," Ami pronounced, but with a focus on an item she found. As Hyki flew off, Ami took a moment to look at the item. T`was shinning very bright but with an attribute of lighting and distance, of only a few feet.

"Awww, just what I need," Ami blurted out.

She somehow slammed it in her pocket but still gently. Doing so, taking took heave of the ground beneath her and rushed off following Hyki to his house. While getting closer to the designated area, running neck and neck Hyki looked to his right, while Ami was on that side as well, and saw something on the other side of the trees running even faster than him plunging into the air and disappearing, when a circling of mechanical machine broke the surroundings. Thus returning to the colorful spew of the sky. When he looked back down-

"Something wrong?" Ami said.

"... Huh, no... see if you can keep up eh?" Hyki yelled as he zoomed off.

"Doubt that!" Ami yelled back.

They soon both arrived at the home of Hyki. Ami had an expression on her face that seemed to resemble a person's face sideways, but at the same time, cocky too.

"Humph... so you made this all by yourself?" said Ami.

"Yep," Hyki said proudly.

"Huu... how did your parents allow you to do this?"

"..."

"Oh, oh no I'm sorry, I didn't know," Ami said nervously watching his head tilt down more and more, then she held him by her side.

"Thank you..." Hyki said as his voice poked, with a blur.

"Humph…" Hyki said this time with a smile, a little push away, and a joke.

"I think we, well mostly you, say too many questions." Hyki gloated.

"Whaa?!?! What is t-

BOOM! BOOM!

Ami and Hyki both saw something in the distance. It was tall and very hard to see, it stood on warning and thought out loud of tiny whispering voices.

"It's another 'Maitonser', and it's probably worse!" Ami said

"I don't care what it is we're taking it down-

Trees of lumber broke down with the intense weight of it. In the process of it coming closer to them, at the same time, their Increasing energy arose from their feet, and to the air above them; transforming their momentum of skill.

"-Together!"

Fight To The Next Journey

Then out of the shadows came a very tall machine made of steal, with a cylinder dome at the top, but with no one in the chair to control the machine. Hyki was angered to know no one was in the chair, this would make it more difficult to figure out who did it or not.

"It must be another trick of Ninga Fu, and I think he has plans for sending this thing," Hyki guessed as a swirly cloud of smoke twirled the top of his head.

In knowing that, he sloshed towards his pockets and yelled out practically scaring Ami herself, to his beeper while looking straight up.

"Calling all close by Teams!" Hyki yelled.

Meanwhile

"Ha! I doubt that ya-
Beep! Beep! Beep!
"Do you think…?"

Rushing away they watched and heard the beeper beep faster following the signals and hearing for noises. Eventually they arrived on time before anything happened. Zooming up came three people, 2 girls and 1 boy. One was spiky haired, thought aggressively, and wore a karate outfit that was a tiny bit too small. Another with Sauvé hair, smooth thinking, was kind of a leader who seemed to want to know what happening. And one other with short smooth hair that's calm, shy voiced, and timid all at the same time thought very wisely wondering what's going on; that's why Hyki answered her first.

"Yes! Bring it on!" yelled the one with spiky hair.

"So what do we have to do first?" said the smooth thinking one.

"Yes, but who are we facing?" said the shy voiced one.

"I can answer all… you first, attack that over there." Hyki pronounced calmly.

But as everyone turned their heads ambition broke from the tip of their heads and slid off. Still the over confident non thinking Penn, balled his fists. Ami, overwhelmed by the tension bent over, held the ground, and tremendously slammed her head through the rock hard dirty ground. They didn't seem to notice that the machine stopped moving.

"Haagh… that's not stopping me!" Penn yelled as the same strength as Hyki's poured through his hands pouncing at the enemy.

"Eeek!" Ami yelped while her head was still underground.

"Yep, figures," "Yep…" Both Hyki and Treeoshe said as Treeoshe hopped on Hyki's shoulders, rubbed his head to watch Penn's ridiculous move. Kiki just stood there confuse as ever about it, looking at Penn.

"It's made of steal and iron," Hyki said.

Baaooinnngggg!

"Ouch…… AWWAAHHH!" Penn screamed.

"Obvious, well, at least he got a dent," Ami said as she plucked her head out of the ground.

BOOM! BOOM!

That woke them out of their conversation.

"…Ha, I shall get my past self, that will help us," Hyki said. Then BAM! Penn rushed towards Hyki as the Booms got louder he knocked over both Treeoshe and Hyki.

"What about my hand?!" Penn yelped.

"… You, o- sorry," Hyki said.

"No, I'm fine. At least I didn't throw my swollen hand at others, knocking me over!" Treeoshe said furiously.

"What?!"

What are we waiting for, let's fight!" Kiki screamed as the others plunged into action while Ami and Hyki stood behind. Soon as Hyki was about to flourish into action, Ami stopped him and reminded him of what he said.

"Wait! Take these designs and ideas, you have to. I made them last night in case I meet you," Ami said.

Without hesitation, Hyki took the designs and went to work as quickly as he could, using tools from the side of his house to work. BAM! Like lightning he was finished. Suddenly The Maitonser swooshed his foot towards Ami, she was stunned at the point. Hyki grabbed her and held the device at the machine.

"What about the others?!" Ami yelped.

"They'll survive! We're going to the past, Ami!" Hyki yelped also.

But behind them was someone in the shadows connected around Ami's arm kinda like string. Click went the button-

SLAWOOSHHH! They went flying out of the air. Something formed around them like electricity in an up oval shape. Silence... closing in, and an enormous vibration quavered the air in circles so big, it was 300 times the planets own size. As the circles move further, it evaporated into space star dust. In twirling winds went both Ami and Hyki, going far away from the planet into light, asleep as their bodies changed. Instead, they popped up in there own bodies.

Waking up quickly, Hyki arose from his long sleep. "Wait, I'm stuck in my past body... and the button's broken." Hyki said looking for Ami, then finding her being swung and thrown so far, she flew miles away, at speeds Hyki could not predict. He saw the machine that did that, so he bald his fist and swung it so hard, he knocked the head off. All the surrounding were quite... dull, and made out of mud. So he rushed to save Ami, by picking up the pieces of button device, then he ran off. Although, he stopped to look back and see that the entire circle area was black and burned, but he had to save Ami.

"Yo, my name is *Penn Hamashe* of team 004 and I'm talking for *Treeoshe Sab* and *Kiki Momorokuni*. So casually I'm walking from time to time. Hyki and I were lying down on a bench and he saw a girl walk and the wind started blowin'; she didn't seem to care, and the girl's skirt went up he and I saw her pa-

BONK!

Owwwww!"

"Ok this is Treeoshe talking now, anyway Hyki ran and ran right, and Ami was so far Hyki couldn't see her. He ran out of breath, so he went to find his old home instead to see if he could contact her. Hyki knows she can handle it."

"...Kiki... um, once he got there, he soon realized that all of his stuff from when he was younger was a little bit out dated, but on his Call-Radio someone answered in to say that Ami was ok, and he could take his time to find where they're at. So he prepared to leave, but he thought... why not take a picture, he might not see this again. So he

took a-a picture of all the rooms in the household, b-because a full life is sometimes…" (All Simultaneously) "… Thought between a photo!"

Meanwhile

When Hyki was growing up, or born, others of society made a ligament that this child would be an unknown child of today, but as Hyki grew older, the friends and others recognize him as a hero instead. So as the rumor spread many people… need his help… Legend Of The Destined One.

"You and I have a lot to learn, about our dreams.... Maybe the one known as "Hyki," could help us."

The Fond Of Memories

"Who was that woman calling me on my Call-Radio?" Hyki said thinking out loud.

"…… My name… you can just call me, Sea…" the Radio responded.

"Huh…?"

"…I can tell you where your friend… Ami is, but only if you wait a couple more weeks though."

"Weeks! Why?! What did you do to her?!" Hyki yelled.

"…Calm down, when I found her she, was crudely damaged, she told me her name and that she was thrown very far…I could tell that it hurt for her to speak."

"Fine then… so, 3 weeks approximately, right?"

"Yes…… oh, and she kept mentioning your name, and how much she missed you, and how much she wanted to ki-…"

SHCCTTCHHERRRCHH! Went the Call-Radio.

"What, What was she telling you!?" Hyki screeched yelling into the Call-Radio speak box, hoping for another answer to come.

Then and there, went the Radio signal gone dead leaving Hyki with no chance of contacting Sea or Ami… for now. After picking up his supplies, he headed out and started looking around for anything that could be a clue towards finding Ami faster. Still, looking around, he couldn't find anything to as even a single clue to finding Ami; just rocks and tall trees.

Suddenly then after, he saw some people he recognized, 2 people. One that seemed to have his own street personality, having street clothes all over. He wore many things like: he had on a red cap that was put on backwards, a pure golden chain with a money sign on it, overly big darkish blue shirt and pants with red shoes. He had on a grill, but his

9

face was innocently different. Thus, the other walking right beside him was a small girl that seemed to be cheerful at the moment. She wore a thick lavender sweater that hung over her hands, two hair holders with smiley faces on them along with ribbons that hung loosely, blue pants and lavender shoes.

Hyki was stunned to see 2 people he hadn't seen before, be so recognizable. He didn't seem to notice he was walking towards them, staring. In doing that, both of them stopped in their tracks, and the street one spoke.

"Yo, half –the-white man," he said in an Arabian voice waving his hands back and forth, and then stopping "What are you doing in our way, coming all up in our grill man?"

"You tell em' dog!" the little girl said sounding terrible.

"…You really need to work on that."

"Um, I'm just trying to find my friend, Ami… have you seen her?"

"Naw man, oooohhaaa! That's it, you really need to SHUT UP!" the street boy yelled.

"Hmhmhm!"

"What, what I do?!……Oh boy, why me?" Hyki yelled, staring at the boy getting uncontrollably angry.

As Hyki pulled out his pole the street boy's face changed into something scary to Hyki. Not in form, but in anger, his eyes bloodshot red, and the rest of the white area of his eye turned completely black, almost completely taking over his face, while the little girl leaned back on a tree smiling as the boy changed. Hyki tried to counter up the same amount of power, but it failed and his pole's electricity was gone. Hyki forgot that he didn't upgrade his pole until he was older. The street boy howled so hard that Hyki's ears and body practically burned away. His teeth turned to daggers when he spoke.

"So, here's your chance, what do you want to say?" the street boy said as his voice turned deeper and more forceful.

"Uhhmm… sorry?" Hyki said mumbling to himself out loud.

"Heh, fine then," said the street boy covering himself yelling as the tension grew, as Hyki couldn't figure out what he was going to do next… and then, with the boy releasing the energy, it fell onto the ground in stars, smiling at Hyki as though he had been happy for the first time. His eyes turned from red to blue.

Hyki was confused, his eyes were dark brown before; and then the girl walked up beside the street boy smiling too.

"Thank you, that's all I wanted to hear from somebody... for so long," said the street boy as he tried to stop tears from coming down his face.

"We're looking for someone too... what's your name?" said the little girl.

"Hyki, Hyki Momoshe's the name."

Taking notice of the conversation, the boy walked forward.

"Yo the name's Philip, but you can call me PG... sometimes."

"You can call me, Shing Ming."

"Do you guys mind helping me find my friend as I help to find yours?" Hyki asked.

The 2 both looked at each other as they thought about it, and then looking back decided.

"Sure, but let's make it a promise ok?" Shing said.

"You got it homie?" Philip said putting his arm out.

"Yeah, as a team we venture off to what we don't know, but will surely learn." Hyki said, putting his arm out also, slapping their hands together in a handshake.

"All right! But what about a team name, and we obviously need more members?"

"How bout' Snap?" Hyki guessed.

"Doomp Snap, I dunno?" Philip guessed even harder.

Shing seem to look at them both arguing about it, and then looking into the sky thinking... crying quietly then speaking.

"...Team Love," Shing said.

"No way man!" Philip shouted.

"Think about it, we've been coming up with crappy names so far, give her a chance." Hyki presumed.

Philip seemed not to argue about it much, so they went with it. There they went as a group heading off; until something happened.

"Wait I forgot something, I'll be right back." Shing said rushing off as the 2 kept walking. About 30 seconds later, both Hyki and Philip heard and saw an explosion hearing Shing scream. So they both ran towards it, but Hyki was running faster than Philip could ever run.

"Go on, go on now, and get her!" Philip said gasping for air. So Hyki rushed to the scenery to se that Shing was knocked out cold. He rushed and grabbed her, then looking up to see someone in the shadow of the fire, but before the shadow could say anything, Philip showed up in time.

"Hey Nevaeh! Why back so early?" Philip shouted, as the surroundings silenced on the big grassy field beneath them.

Hyki's Little Pet

"Yello, *Philip Lenchi* of team 003 here, funny thing; I barely got into the team because of the way I acted towards my friends… but man, they taught me everything on how to be nice to others, you know what I'm sayin'? Ya see, what happened was… that… she. Shing, could you take over?"

"Sure dog. See what happened was that after Philip said what he had to say to Nevaeh, she responded by coming out of the fire and showing part of her face. A grin to a heavy smile, then flushing into the air attacking Philip so close that Philip stood scared in his feet. BAM! Hyki came up with his pole, blocking Nevaeh's attack, that seemed to look like daggers in her hands. Then blowing her out of position with one swing of his pole. Still, she seemed to have landed up right, while I started to wake to see it all; barely though. While Hyki got up and started throwing swings at Nevaeh, she threw them back, block-to-block… Philip stood scared… I couldn't stand to see Philip stunned in battle……but… anyway, it was great talking! *Shing Ming* of team 003… Oh yeah, after the fighting continued, it stopped and I stood up to see that they stood exhausted, facing each other."

"So… huh-huh, that's all you got… huh-huh?" Hyki demonstratively said as he pointed his pole at Nevaeh and then plopping back to his kneecaps, bending over gasping for air. Hyki never realized how much the pole would take out of you when it's not up graded, but how much power it could put on the enemy.

"… No… but I know-…" Nevaeh said looking up then vanishing in a streaking cloud of dark black darkness.

"Hyki… I have a debt to pay…"

Hyki stood up surprised to notice that she sounded kinda like the woman on the Call-Radio. Then he looked down to see Shing was a little hurt.

"Oh Shing are you alright? Philip, take Shing back to my place, here." Hyki said throwing him a map.

"…Huh? Oh yeah," Philip said taking Shing onto his arms as Shing smiled looking up at Philip.

"Wait what about you?" Philip said turning around.

"I gotta do something… something."

"……Alright, see ya man," said Philip walking back with a concern.

Hyki walked by across the field to the other side, not even thinking about what happened just a few minutes before. He kept walking and walking thinking about the whereabouts of Ami. Suddenly, he stumbled too far to see someone lying on the ground. Alarmed, ran to the person to heave to, but only to see a girl and a note.

This girl you see before you is different and must be taken care of. Maybe if you could teach her the right thing, maybe certain things, would happen. You will be only able to see Ami, until you can come see; don't worry, I heard rumors about it. Plus she gets impressed with boys like you.

"Huh? What does this person mean by different?" Hyki wondered.

The girl had arisen from her sleep. Only parts of her body were showing. It seemed that she wasn't wearing any clothes but the brown cloth over her. She stared at Hyki with an indecisive expression as Hyki gazed back surprised. She lifted part of her body up making her ears show. Hyki half-way blushed, and then looked again to see something.

"Whaa! You're a c-c-… some kind of cat girl?!" Hyki said as the girls tail flopped up and down while she smiled. He looked to see that she had very-somewhat tan skin, brown hair, and a long brown tail.

She didn't seem to fight back, so Hyki carried her, and decides to take the weird creature home. When walking her home, she didn't say a word, wrapping her long tail around his waist. Hyki still blushed as she made herself feel comfortable being carried. Getting back, walking through the door, Philip spoke while putting bandages on Shing.

"Congrats on the new girlfriend homie!"

"She was just abandoned alone… I'll take care of her for a while," Hyki said with a fear in his voice heading up the stairs. He quickly feeds her, so her energy is a bit better. She's still weak, so he nervously exchanges her clothes for a pair of his own clothes so he can helplessly give her a bath. Hyki has still yet to know that she is still conscious about everything. Then out of the open, she pops up to thank Hyki for helping her, by giving him a little dance.

"Givie cute boy a kitty dance," proclaimed the mysterious Cat Girl.

"Oh… hmhmhm… you're welcome," said Hyki. But after giving her back her towel and embracing her to keep her warm, a bad bad omen was coming from her. Still, she had that same smile, but something was wrong, but at the same time, right? What? Night fall had come, the others slept in the extra rooms, while the girl slept in with Hyki, and Hyki wanted to get some shut eye. So he quickly turned of the light and went to sleep. He heard something in the middle of the night.

He got up to see that it was the girl meowing like a cat.

"Huh… what's wrong, something you want?" Hyki wondered as she pointed at her collar.

"Oh… that's just a collar."

"Meow!" she said aggressively and loudly.

"Alright, Alright… I'm coming!" Hyki said as he got off his bed and looked at the collar closely. The girl was very tall so she looked down at Hyki. Then suddenly the girl pressed Hyki's head towards her breasts and purred like a real cat. Overwhelmed backed up blushing while the girl looked up, confused; it's her way of saying thank you. She showed Hyki something in her hand that seemed to look like a tape recorder and a tape recorder tape. He started playing it and listened, but it was plugged into the girls arm as a source of power.

Hello, I'm just here for the show, so please, if you ever want to see this pathetic girl again with memory and all, you'll do as I say.

"And what if I don't?" Hyki pondered about.

You'll never see you friend Ami again… I know how much she means to you. So at the end of your 3 days, abandon this girl or else I'll get Ami destroyed my self……

The recorder went blank, as the girl started to crawl away.

"Hello?!…… hey "Meowshe" come here"

"Meow," she said putting the recorder back and getting comfortable where Hyki sat.

"Do you know where Ami is?"

She pointed out the window as Hyki also looked to see someone in the shadows at the tip of the mountain running soon as Hyki saw it. Rushing out the door came Hyki exhausted and tired but still running after the shadow. Finally catching up to it, he spoke.

"Wait…" Hyki said then being knocked out by exhaustion; fell asleep as the shadow slowly faded from his eyes.

The next day, day 2, Hyki slowly woke up out of his sleep, tried, yawning and stretching his arms, but heard giggling in the background.

"…Wha?!" Hyki screamed as Meowshe was sleeping right up on top of him, and Philip and Shing were laughing manically. Meowshe woke up to see she was on top of him… so she blushed smiled and meowed loudly sitting up.

"…Purr…Meow!" she said as though she actually liked it.

They both again laughed even louder.

"Congrats on the new girl, so what's ya secret man?" Philip asked.

"She is not my girlfriend!"

"So she really likes you… she could want to be your pet!" Shing said.

"..Ok, that's it, I'm telling you one thing, she's not my pet!"

"Meow, mow, mow!" Meowshe said as though she were saying *'Yes I am!'*

"Alright… we put her on you on purpose and-

"No we didn't man," Philip said.

"We didn't?"

"No…"

They both laughed again.

"You must've done somethin' to er man."

16

"No I didn't!" Hyki yelled.

"Well anyway, Breakfast is down stairs… man, you have a lot of food dog!" Shing said horribly.

"I'm telling you, you really need to work on that," Philip said as both of them walked downstairs.

Our Quest

Hyki quickly got up and got all of his equipment as he busted out the window running into the forest. After he got there, he thought to himself.

"There's gotta be something as to where I can save both, Ami and Meowshe..." Hyki said out loud. Suddenly he heard Meowshe in the distance.

"Meo-... ma-... H-Hyki!" Meowshe screamed.

In riddled with appreciation, he rushed to Meowshe only to see that she was somehow trapped by wolves. Thrusting himself into action stood in front of Meowshe with his arms wide across. Then by taking one arm, pointed his pole strait up.

ZANGGAERAAP! Went the tip of the pole with its power of electricity scaring all the wolves away.

"Are you ok?" Hyki said draping his arm to his side.

"Meow..." Meowshe said dragging him into a nearby cave and petting him until he felt better. Hyki fell asleep then after. The light glistened on the 2 of them softly.

Hyki woke up later to see Meowshe was on him, again, while he lent against the wall. Hyki didn't react by blushing. Meowshe seemed to have managed to get some food from his place, as she held it in front of his face. She grabbed some of the food with her mouth and fed it to Hyki; he still didn't react. She wore something different this time: she had on a silky-smooth t-shirt that had a shine on its exterior, light-brown shorts, light-brown boots, and some dark-brown gloves with a blackish shiny exterior.

"Me-Meowshe can-n't stands to s-see y-you afraid..." She said as her stomach grumbled.

Hyki grabbed some of the food, and fed it to Meowshe. She purred at Hyki, as she stared at him with a glare of wanting. Then, Philip seemed to have popped up along with Shing. And there Meowshe stood up and pointed out the cave opening Meowshe sensed something in the distance, while they all saw it. Something that was dark in pure daylight, was something that seemed to look very angry but calm. Its body black as space, but eyes white all over. It pointed its hand at us, a black whole seemed to come out of his hand and flushed them in an enormous explosion that knocked them and the cave clear off the ground flying at speeds they couldn't count, of the air, as it followed running the same beneath them.

Hyki was in front while the others flew in back uncontrollably. Hyki looked down to see a claw coming out the shadows hand, like a claw of purple blackness, and it grabbed Shing down slamming her to the bare field below them, as the Shadow still ran beneath them. Then Philip as well, while Hyki couldn't see his friends as he yelled out their names.

"Philip! Shing!" Hyki shouted as his chances for anyone to hear him are dim.

He looked back at Meowshe to see she was shouting his name. The shadow began to reach for Meowshe as Hyki started to hear what Meowshe was saying to herself.

"Not in case of War let it rain sun…"

"…Oh no, not this time…!" Hyki said to himself as he reached for his pole, pointing it at the shadow releasing forms of electrical waves blasting it towards the shadow, stopping it in its tracks. Hyki also stopped it from grabbing Meowshe. Hyki pointed his pole down and blasted it to catch up to Meowshe, and grabbing her safely back down to the ground. While partially using his older version of his jetpack, he also didn't get to upgrade it. The shadow, still alive, stood confidently staring at both Meowshe and Hyki. Lifting its picture, pointed its finger at them.

"I've been hired to delete you…" said the shadow.

"What is wrong with you, you blasting us into complete air, hurting my friends…" a pause then a thought out loud, "You've been hired by Ninga fu… or even that shadow in the dark, I saw last night, that was you, wasn't it?!?" shouted Hyki.

"…No… think about it"

Stumbling in his words thought to him self and miraculously came to a conclusion.

"......Are you a Clone?" Hyki said curiously.

"...In some ways... yes... no... you should know something by now..."

"What...?" Hyki said as he braced his pole.

The shadow swung his arms and shoulders side to side and spoke as he began to float. The grass beneath him swerved in a circular motion.

"I do not promise this... pain" the shadow said as both Hyki and Meowshe plunged into the shadows face. Hyki was surprised to see that Meowshe was joining.

"Th-The, Thuis, This is *Meowshe Vocu* sa-saying of t-the bu-bu, ba, battle Hyki with me h-had. T-The sh-..." "Do you want me to take over?" "Mow..." "Ok so the shadow in front of us is plunging into us... I'm actually surprised to see that Meowshe can fight. And you know what, I think I might not spoil it for you, you can figure it out."

Our Match

At the last peak of attack the shadow drew the claw out again, as while Hyki did the same, by putting his pole strait out by his side.

BOOM!!!

The clash of the 2 forms of weapons splashed in to the air. Meowshe rushed to the back of the shadow and pointed her hand into the air. Her hand's fingernails grew 4 times their size, sharp as nails to the point. Hyki saw Meowshe and spoke with impressments as he still struggled.

"Huh, huh… alright, Meowshe!" Hyki said breathing heavily.

Meowshe drew back her hand and thrashed it directly down the shadows back. It went completely through the shadow, like as though if it were some kind of hologram. The shadow turned its head and stared at Meowshe. Then with a frail disturbing look of anger, and then a freaky smile, the shadow's hand that was blocking Hyki's pole, turned red; blasting Hyki into the other side of the field into a cloud of grass and smoke. Turning back to Meowshe, it struck her, and slashed her, leaving scares, while it was still attacking her. Way on the other side of the field was Hyki actually not hurt.

"Owww! Wait, where's Meowshe, where'd she go?" Hyki said as he stumbled trying to catch up to Meowshe.

Hyki ran over to see the shadow was staring at him and then running off.

"Hey! You're not getting away so easily!" Hyki yelled as Meowshe shouted his name. He stumbled to go see what was wrong.

"Hyki!!!… nugh… Hyki!!!" Meowshe screamed.

Once Hyki got to Meowshe he saw that her clothes were torn off to shreds, eyes wide open, and she spoke with no signs of damage anywhere on her body, clean.

"Don't l-let him a-a-attack you Hyki…"

"……W-What?"

"His p-pain is y-yours w-when he a-attacks…"

Hyki thought and then reacting to Meowshe's wants for help, and then aiding the others to... let's just say, they were badly damaged.

The next day, day 3, Philip and Shing were awakened at Hyki's house by Meowshe speaking through the outside of the door, of their room.

"Huh...... aww man Shing, wake up wake up!" Philip said.

"Wha-What... wait weren't we just in a fight?" Shing asked.

"Yeah... wait, listen... is that that cat girl Hyki was hangin' out with?"

"Yep..."

There, Meowshe came bursting through the door yelling about how Hyki was gone, and with no way of finding him. They seemed to notice that Meowshe was dazing off, thinking about something.

Flashback For Meowshe Moments Ago:

Meowshe woke up in Hyki's bed startled with fear, but with a focus to her senses. Her neck seemed itchy, so she looked to see a photo of some sort. It was a picture of notes Hyki had to written to Meowshe. Soon as she some how miraculously read the note she understood quickly what she had to do.

Afterwards She Awoke From Her Flashback

"Hey, where are you going girl?" Philip asked.

"I'm g-going f-f-for a walk-k" Meowshe responded.

Meowshe quickly took what she had to take and headed out of the house.

Meanwhile

Hyki was struggling trying to keep up with all of his energy, walking out of the forest in to sand-like plain. When he got closer and closer, he saw three things in one area which seemed completely off bound: A couple mountains forming, a drifting island, and the rest like a desert with a small base in the distance. Hyki started to approach this area, and saw someone actually gliding across the ground of sand... It was someone he knew, it was... Treeoshe Hyki would think to himself. She came up with a whirlwind of sand behind her and stopped in front of Hyki, but with a suspicious look on her face, yet angry for not knowing Hyki.

"Hey, your not in a good mood what are you doing out here… ya know, I think I've been here before… yeah I have" Hyki said with a sign of good nature.

The girl looked at him, as he talked, as if she were saying 'who are you?!?' out loud. She had perfectly dark purple dyed hair as thought it were real. She wore mechanical-like shoes that may have provided her to glide across the sand. On her arms she wore torn sleeves, and as for her shirt, it looked perfectly normal, but a bit short in a purple-like color. Treeoshe seemed to respond quickly and eagerly to everything Hyki had said to her.

"Oh and before I forget, did you see a girl going by the name Ami, Treeoshe? with p-pink hair, hehe… sorry when ever I hear-

"Who are you…?" Treeoshe said fast.

"What, it's me Hyki."

"If you'd like to visit one of us ask now… these are our grounds, and we're willing to protect it…" Treeoshe said fast again.

"Huh…? Did you, no, do you remember me?" Hyki wondered.

"…No but I'd be happy to make you something to drink at my place…" Treeoshe said with a side of confusion in her voice and face.

"……Ok, you sure…?"

"Come on you can meet the others and tell me all about it…" Treeoshe said as both of them eventually came to a stop at a small base. Hyki took a look at all the 3 different kinds of places put into one, beforehand.

"Well this is my base"

"This small thing is your base?"

"I thought you might say that" Treeoshe said leaning herself onto Hyki's shoulders with eagerness. She pulled herself back up, and pulled out some sort of button from her backpack. She pressed it… the ground barely shook but forms sand struck the small base. It grew and grew taller wider, all forms and sizes. Finally after it was finished, it seemed a little authentic, but it was a base, sort of like a ship of some kind Hyki would think to himself.

Looking For A Close Friend

After both Treeoshe and Hyki got a broad look at everything, Treeoshe pointed at all 3 of the areas from left to right.

"Over there to the left is Penn's area, he trains a lot so try not to get in his way try to come when he's in his 'little hut,' but knock, he's a bit perverted I caught him once looking at me while I was taking a-

WHHAAAAAHH WHHAAAAAHH went an alarm coming from Treeoshe's tower tip point.

"Wha-What's going on?!?"

"An intruder has hit the premises at alarming speeds! Come on we have to get out of the alarm grounds!" Treeoshe said as she zoomed back to her base.

Then out of nowhere in rows out of the sand came large lasers aiming at whatever was in sight.

"…Wait, that's, that's Meowshe! I gotta save her" Hyki screamed.

"No, you'll get blasted away!" Treeoshe said but it was too late, Hyki went of as the lasers tried to blast him away as well.

Meanwhile

Meowshe came running at the lasers shouting Hyki's name looking for him with the sight of cry in her eyes, but with a rhythm of a heart beat. Suddenly, by the mountain side a splash of lava sprouted out from between the wedges of the mountains, like a dart in the air except that dart was a boy. As for the other side the same thing happened only this time it was a girl and made of water from the place of ancient, hanging onto one thread of rock. They both came rushing at Meowshe trying to attack her. Hyki, still running, saw behind him the two of them coming at him and Meowshe.

"No!" Hyki yelled as he put his pole into the air trying to block the enemy's attack. Something surprising happened, a second pole popped in his hands, not magically, but formed from the energy in his hands and heart.

"Huh... a second pole, but it's-

Interrupted by the pounding of the two that were coming after them, Hyki didn't understand why this 1 pole blocked both of them. Plashing back away from Hyki, the two both charged back to strike again.

Afterwards

Treeoshe ran to the alarm security switch, and slammed her had down on it turning the large lasers off. They stopped seeing that Treeoshe had screamed for the two to stop. Meowshe still stunned woke from the daze and swarmed around Hyki against the firer-like one. Penn, tried to attack him; his face was so covered, not by the hair, no, but the extreme shadows. Still all he did was turn his face and slammed his elbow back knocking Meowshe out cold as the other water girl was shocked to see this action. The clone of water flushed to the ground, disappearing.

Later then in that day, Hyki and Treeoshe were talking about Hyki's confusion while walking through Treeoshe's sight hall.

"So you really 'really' don't remember me?" Hyki said with even more curiosity.

"Nope... but you do seem like a person I would really like to know myself. By the way, trying to protect your friend, and the way she goes the distance to find you, continuously" Treeoshe said specifically, "Does she have any passion or zeal for you ever since you came across her as to being a friend?"...

At The Same Time

With a headache in her forehead Meowshe awoke with a faint look and then plopped down, put her eyes wide open and shot up, noticing she was on a bed; an empty room. Panicking that Hyki wasn't in her sight, screamed. Hyki could hear her far away, at any moment. He rushed as Treeoshe followed.

"Where is she?" Hyki wondered as he ran throughout the halls randomly.

"In the infirmary!" she shouted, "follow me!"

"Right... let's go!" Hyki yelled.

Once they reached the door, they both saw the door bang... then suddenly stop... Opening the door they saw Meowshe holding someone in her arms.

"Look Hyki… this is … Ami" Meowshe said.

Stunned looked at Ami, but something was wrong. Heat like vibrations came off of Ami and Meowshe as both Hyki and Treeoshe looked. The tape recorder started playing again.

Hello again, it's been a long time since we last talked huh…don't forget, your precious girlfriend is still along and well…keep it together will you… with our deal…by the way, my friend here keeps dreaming about you every day… hahaha… make a choice.

Soon after, the weird vibrations vanished along with the "Ami," that seemed to be there, Treeoshe spoke aloud.

"…Hyki you seemed to have recognized this… this… that thing, what-

When Treeoshe turned her head she saw agony and sadness, anger and pain on Hyki's face all in one emotion. Tears ran down his face as he stared at the arms of Meowshe; an explosion of emotion blurred his vision, and Hyki fell to the floor first to his knees, then onto Meowshe's stomach and cried.

"Why do they always have to separate us!?!" Hyki cried out as both Treeoshe and Meowshe stared.

"Every time we have the time to sit down and talk to each other, Ninga Fu has to rattle things up again!" said this time with aggression.

"…… you know, things can be made if focused…" Treeoshe added.

"Huh…?"

"M-My f-f-feelings for you are… h-heart Hyki… heart" Meowshe said as she looked down at Hyki with a perky smile with tears flowing from hers to Hyki's face, as Hyki looked back. "Meowshe t-thinks t-that you are m-m-my best friend, a-and you s-shouldn't giv-ve in to h-his w-ways any more, b-but she h-hasn't g-given u-up y-yet on you yet Hyki. D-D-Don't s-stop being the a-adv-venturous boy Meowshe h-has come t-to know…" Meowshe said, as Hyki came to see not how much she adored him as a friend but as a love instead, and a smile came back at Meowshe as it clearly wiped off Hyki's face.

"……You know your right!"

"Huh, Meowshe d-doesn't understand?"

Hyki quickly got up off of Meowshe and shot up, and slammed both Treeoshe and Meowshe on the bed; pointing his fingers at them both almost knocking them back on the bed-

"Set all your belongings and equipment ready, were off to save Ami!" Hyki shouted, while Treeoshe and Meowshe looked at each other, and thus a smile grew on both their faces. Suddenly they jumped out off the bed and pointed at Hyki-

"Fine I'll get my friends to come along too! Treeoshe shouted.

"And were off!" Meowshe continued afterwards.

They both busted through the door as they called their teammates names out loud, while Hyki only walked out the door, with a smile on his face. When Hyki got to the tip of the window, he placed his palm on the window seal and uttered to himself.

"Ami, even though our hearts are separated, we shall never break in pieces no more. So, Ami, until then... don't forget our promise... and... ya gotta tell me what happened!" Hyki blurted afterwards, heading out the building to meet his new acquaintances, for his new adventure.

Chapter (002):

The Boundary Line

Hyki stood out in the open, with Meowshe following, and then cuddling right next to him outside. Silence was in the air as Treeoshe came out slowly with an utterly happy face through the sliding doors, walking up to them, spoke.

"I'd like you to meet the team…!" Treeoshe said striking the air with jerky emotion, as silence soon converted to tiny rumbles. As like before, a splash of lava sprouted out from between the wedges of the mountains, like a dart in the air except, and that dart was the same boy. And yet again another pole, looking exactly alike, appeared.

"……So ya wanna fight huh? Again, we fight?!!" Hyki said pondering in his yelling.

"Wha-? Penn stop messing with our new friend…" Treeoshe pronounced in a calm voice-like gesture. She put her left hand above her head, and as soon as the boy came close to Hyki over her head, she was able to grab him and slam him to the ground.

The boy got up, plucking his head from out of the ground, "What was that for?!" the boy said with anguish. Hyki looked at him at noticed all of his features and recognized him easily. His hair stood up with red and orange, in a spiky formation. He had a white shirt that was too small, and white pants that were too big, but a red belt that was just right. His hair was too big to see his eyes, still, the rest of his skin stood out in a fuzzy peach color. What he always forgot was his shoes. Thus Hyki thought, Yep that's Penn alright.

"So what's with the second… uhh, pole thing" Treeoshe asked in a ponder-like confusion as the pole dissolved into Hyki's hands.

"How can you be so calm when you just slammed your teammate

into the ground?" Hyki blurted out as his adrenalin cooled, "Wait......
you said team…" he pondered.

"…So…" Treeoshe answered as though she even found herself
dumfounded.

"…Well, shouldn't there be another too?" Hyki enforced in
question.

Silence drifted through the air as Treeoshe had a concerned face.

"Oh… you mean Kiki… she's not been so good lately… she's been
in her little temple place a lot lately" Treeoshe pronounced, "We haven't
been able to get to her either!" Penn added as Treeoshe dragged him
back to her side.

"You seem the right type to get to her… go cheer her up, we'll be
right here"

"Not unless I-

BONK!!! Treeoshe stopped him in his tracks pounding him on his
head.

Hyki was confused at first, but he soon got the clue. Hyki jogged
towards the temple while Meowshe stood by, letting him go easily, as
Treeoshe looked back and said out loud to herself-

"I sure hope she'll listen to this one…"

Hyki got closer to the temple to notice again the one-thread rock. It
was so fragile, he would think. He turned to his left and saw Treeoshe's
place was set up, in a way, where he can run up the wall and jump
onto the temple. He backed up and took full speed at the wall, and fell
completely to his face to the sand. Treeoshe saw him trying and said in
her mind-

"Oh, no…" as Hyki fell making her more uncomfortable.

Boom! "No…"

Boom! "No, No!"

BOOM! "Hyki focus…!"

This time Hyki plopped his head and walked away a distance, and
then plopping to the sand beneath him. Treeoshe had an almost crying
face; Meowshe was no different. They all stared at Hyki but he got into
a funny trackers start position.

WWHHOOOOSHHH! His backpack took form of a jet, while
both Treeoshe and Meowshe cheered with a uplifting face of joy, Hyki
thrashed up the wall with a little smirk on his face running unbelievably

fast with his legs, pounced off the wall and landed on the temple with a 'humph' and a smile as the girls cheered on. He turned around and saw that his shoes were on grass... grass Hyki thought. He looked up to see ruins that were peaceful, as a feeling rose into his lungs; he could see practically everything up here. Hyki shook his head and focused were to find Kiki. He saw a hole in the side of the ruins and heard tiny weeping. Hyki slowly walked over to the hole to see a girl crying with such long hair he couldn't see even the color of her hair, it looked very dark blue. Hyki bent down with a worried face as he tried to come closer.

"Go away!" Kiki screeched with such a voice; Hyki could tell that she was very shy.

"But I..." Hyki responded.

"I said, GO AWAY!"

Hyki plopped all the way to his bottom and sat, leaned against the wall, and stared at the view.

"Ya know... I'm lonely too..."Hyki continued as Kiki turned her head very slowly to look at Hyki.

"I've been through so much, had so many fights, discovered new things... new... discoveries, new loves, and adventures that always get to me," A tear ran down his face-

"Oh, wait... you're cry- interrupted Hyki went on.

"I never thought I'd meet anyone who was willing stop in place for... for... just to let it all out, when you should rather spend it all with your love, your friends... hope..." but right after Hyki stopped, Kiki spoke grabbing onto his back, squeezing Hyki tightly so close it looked as though she were on his back.

"But I n-never had anyone... not give up on me like that! .... When I was a girl I was considered the wimp, but I progressed, and AGAIN pushed down. I had to run away form it all, I had to, so I came here to let my stress go... but now that we've met, I want to do better!" Kiki stopped in her tracks to see a smile on his face.

"Let's go..."

"Huh?" Kiki murmured.

Hyki stood up to still have her on his back, and walked out of the hole.

"Show me how you look eh?"

Kiki got off Hyki and clutched her arms together, blushing heavily, a frown, as Hyki turned around to see her.

"What no smile… show me the real Kiki?" Hyki said happily.

A big blank face soon turned into a huge smile.

"Right on!" Hyki yelped as he observed her. Her cheeks were always a-faded rouge, her hair hung down to her knees of a natural color white. Her skin almost the color of her hair bristles lightly, pale short blue jeans and pale long sleeve red shirt. Still, her eyes stood out bright green. Reaching in his back pack, he took her picture, as the blushing grew heavier.

"Let's not hold back anymore, let's meet our new adventure" Hyki said in a dim voice.

Meanwhile

"…He sure is taking a long time in there…" Treeoshe said wondrously.

Penn got in front of Treeoshe looking protective, "The silence is getting too proactive..... huh?"

"I can stand for myself you know" Treeoshe said as she forced her eyes up.

They stood in silence. Meowshe started to back away very slowly.

"I-Is Hyki going t-to be o-o-ok?" Meowshe said with such fear that it seemed that she started to cry.

Suddenly a streak of colors came off Kiki's temple and landed in the sand leaving an explosion in the sand. The others didn't know what or who it is. Then standing up, stood Hyki with Kiki smiling on his back. All cheery, accept for Meowshe who cheered halfway, and with an empty face. Meowshe bent down and pounced towards Hyki then stopped immediately still on the ground, staring at Kiki.

"Who's t-this Hyki?" Meowshe said with a concern still staring at Kiki. Kiki started to frown and hide behind Hyki's back more, "Uh… Hyki…"

"Oh, Meowshe this is Kiki… friends of Treeoshe and Penn, and Kiki this is Meowshe, I found her abandoned in the Alco forest.

"H-Hi…" Kiki said shyly.

"Hi," Meowshe said quickly as though her speech improved a bit.

"Well nothing's going to stop us now… we have all our equipment, now lets head out to the *Boundary Line*!" Treeoshe blurted out.

"Yeah, let's go!" Hyki followed in.

So all headed out as one using their own abilities, and even Philip and Shing joined the run soon after. The afternoon came near as they came to a stop, at a large crevice Treeoshe called the Boundary line, and the group decided to take a five minute break. A long dirt road stood as on one side Hyki sat with Kiki on his shoulder, with Meowshe next to them, staring at Kiki. While next to her, the group conversed with each other.

"Phew… It's good to run real fast once in a while" Hyki said blurting his words out deliberately. Hyki looked at Meowshe staring at Kiki in an up most scary face.

"Meowshe, why are you staring at Kiki like that?"

A long pause then she spoke, "Because, t-the way s-she's h-holding you Hyki……" she spoke again but this time with an angry voice echoing her thoughts of feeling, "Hyki's mine! Why do you have to take him away from me?! I want Hyki to love me not YOU!"

Everyone stopped laughing and looked over at the commencing conversation. Meowshe took her hand back then forced it forward at Kiki, knocking Hyki out of the way. Luckily, Kiki had blocked her attack with a shield of water. Hyki got up, but this time he had a scratch on his face that bled; making Meowshe upset, then furious with anger.

"H-Hyki…" saying first at a soft voice, "…OOOOGGHH! KNOW LOOK WHAT YOU'VE DONE! PREPARE YOURSELF, THIS IS IT!" her voice bellowed again as though the tape recorder was talking.

Everyone this time, started to get up. Meowshe's face grew unheedingly angry, but soft again as the tape recorder voice grew out of Meowshe's body, and into a solid formation shadow.

"His pain is yours when he attacks…" Meowshe said as her eyes formed dull, pouting her head down.

The Boundary Line Is Nothing!

Hyki suddenly remembered Meowshe saying that and then said it softly to himself, "His pain… is yours… when he attacks…" He would think, what an obvious line, but there must be more.

HHHAAAAAAUGGGGHHHHHHHH! The shadow roared in a scary voice, while Meowshe fell helplessly to the ground.

He thought about it for a sec, but every one had already hopped into action, attacking the shadow.

Hyki said it again; "His pain… is yours… when he attacks…" the shadow's huge hand came rushing at Hyki, flipping him upon the tip of a tree. Hyki stopped and looked at the clouds flow…… BAM! Hyki understood in an instant.

"Everyone, secure it to the ground!" Hyki yelped, jumping off the tree, grabbing Meowshe taking her across the Boundary Line, as Kiki followed.

The group used their own abilities, being able to secure the shadow. When Hyki and Meowshe crossed the Boundary Line, the tape recorder broke, having the shadow yelp heavily allowed. The group stared at it shrivel up, vanishing into stars.

Hyki flashed back remembering a promise

"So no matter what we go through, and conflicts we have, well always be friends, right?" "No matter what…"

"And promise me if we separate, cut a lock of your hair and point it the way you are"

"Haha, Promise…"

Coming back looked at Meowshe open her eyes

"Meowshe's f-free… Meowshe can f-finally l-l-love" Meowshe said pouring tears out of her eyes. Hyki looked down at her in his arms crying as well, "The fool never thought that he could've been separated from you…"

The others stared then smiled at them crying. Hyki sat Meowshe down, wiped away his tears and slammed his finger into the air.

"We're off to find Ami!"

"Well, where in the world, do we all go first?!" Penn said confused. "We have the entire continent to search, and we don't have the slightest a-clue. And need I remind you, we've got plans too!"

"…Heh, follow me, I got an idea!" Hyki pronounced waving his hand toward the direction he was heading. Everyone followed. While running up the hill, Meowshe looked at Kiki beside her and apologized.

"S-Sorry for h-hitting you K-Kiki…"

"It's ok, y-you never m-meant to…" Kiki said smiling back.

They both smiled at each other catching up with the others. Once everyone got to the top, Hyki saw a lock of Ami's hair shaped like an arrow pointing towards more flat grassed lands. He also saw mud-like pillars again. So he put the lock of hair in his pocket and grabbed out his camera.

"Say cheese!"

"CHEESE!"

Afterwards

'The People' are looking at the girl, but talk to each other.

"So, should we allow her to go to the boy, Hyki, yet?"

"Yes she'll carry out the mission."

"Do you think she'll revolt, and rat us out?"

"I don't know… not yet…"

"Hey this is Zuman Claw again to tell you what happened. So the group ran down the hill, finding more locks of hair. Hyki looked back to see he found the dull muddy area again just like before… like a circle, and just like before; colors spewed of mechanical things. The group, or "Team Love", decided to sleep for the night across in the grassy area. Hyki stared at the stars, while the other slept in groups, Hyki slept with both Kiki and Meowshe curled beside him. A bit weird for me but he said to himself 'Just wait Ami… I'm coming…'"

Hyki's Commin' Open A New Book And Fly

Afterwards

The next day, all of them began to awaken, in start of a new day. The grass on the field blew smoothly as the warming wind passed. Clouds of white bloomed firmly, like lilies in the spring.

"Pack it up… were moving on!" Hyki yelped.

Kiki was on the side of Hyki, pulling down on his shirt. "W-What do we do if we get lost, huh?

"No need to worry…" He said as he started to walk forward. "I remember the times we had playing with those things… but when everyone… forgot…" Then a pause came into his voice.

"Are you alright?!" Kiki said loudly. Everyone started to turn their heads to see Hyki, so they all rushed over, and blurted out questions of worry to see if Hyki was alright.

"……If only…" Hyki said very softly.

"If only you had friends like us, uhh when you where little right?" Penn said.

All agreed out loud.

"We'll put a world a-hurt for anyone who tries to get in the way of dis friendship!" Philip said.

"Does it hurt inside when you can't get to your dream, your goal! Does it hurt?!" Hyki flourished loudly. Everyone had a sorrowful face in the process, so all gathered around Hyki and gave him a hug, very slightly rocking him.

Philip started to talk in a more calm voice. "Yeah it may hurt, but you have to have a source of strength, otherwise you won't be able to cry."

Hyki eyes popped out, and then he knew what was wrong.

Afterwards, he got up and had walkie-talkies in his hands.

"These were used in with my other battles… but you guys can use them, so we can never be apart."

Everyone was given one and looked up at Hyki worried.

"Well… my dreams are waiting…" Philip said softly, "Let's go Shing!"

"Kay!" Shing beeped out loud, as she ran beside Philip.

"I'm off, see you…later" Philip said starting to run off, but was stopped in his tracks.

"Hey, don't forget about us!" Hyki yelped.

Philip turned slightly; you could only see the side of his right eye, "You're all a part of my dream yo!" Philip bellowed as he ran off further and further beyond the grass.

"Well we're of too to finish our research, Hyki." Treeoshe said grabbing Penn by the waist, pulling him close to her side making Penn blush uncontrollably. They ran off in the opposite direction.

Hyki grew a big smile, but had a weary face. Hyki turned around and spoke.

"Well, it's just the 3 of us now." Hyki placed his hand down as the two looked puzzled.

"Team Love…?" Hyki said smiling.

The both put their hands on his hand and repeated simultaneously, "Team Love!"

"Kiki here… uhh, oh yeah, we took off Hyki used his rocket thing, while I carried Meowshe with using my water ability. We f-flew very high, where the clouds were. But something happened when I looked at Hyki as he looked down below the clouds. I remember him saying something, "It can't be…" so then he p-plummeted towards land as Meowshe and I followed. Because a full life is sometimes… Thought between a photo!"

"What do you see!?" Kiki said wondrously loud.

"…"

"Well, what do you see Hyki!?" Kiki said again loud.

WHHOOOSSSSSHHHHHH! A sound both Meowshe and Kiki could here themselves. Having to see Hyki plummet to the surface;

they could see the wind bounce off too. They followed him as fast as they could.

"You guys head off that way until I give the signal for ya'll to come out!" Hyki said pointing his arms in directions as he yelled.

"W-What does t-that mean!?" Meowshe responded heavily, but lightly.

"Go now!" Hyki yelped, as they both headed towards bushes nearby to hide.

Hyki slammed to the ground by a tree were it made his face not seen, making the girl with pink hair turn. She had died pink hair in a pony-tail spiked up, yellow shirt and blue pants, along with pink and white shoes. The girl was much injured in a way, being alarmed, flushed out a heavy worn stick at Hyki and spoke.

"Who are you?"

"…Ami… I…"

"How do you know my name huh? You got a lot a nerve kid… Have you seen a boy named Hyki around? I assume you're the type of person who'd know anyone around."

Hyki walked forward out of the shadows of the tree, to see his eyes wide open, staring at Ami. Ami suddenly did the same, dropping her stick into the dirt-like sand. Hyki pulled out the strands of hair from his pocket. "I remembered." Silence arouse between the 2 finding each other again, smiled, running towards each other and embracing with tears of joy and sorrow. Time passed as they began to fall still holding each other, pink pedals fell; later, letting, go. A while after, as the crying began to seize, Meowshe and Kiki came out with worried faces.

"Hyki o-ok?" Meowshe said crawling upon the grass.

"Who are they… friends?" Ami pondered.

"This is the team I traveled with all this time, 'Team Love,'" Hyki said getting up and pointing at them.

"This is Kiki…"

"Hello… Ami." Said Kiki

"And this is Meowshe…"

"H-Hi!" Said Meowshe

"Not much of a talker is she? Let alone her-… Ami rushed over to Meowshe and started poking her ears, "Is she some type a… a, cat girl thing?" Ami shouted.

"Weird conspiracy huh?" Hyki responded.

After a while, Meowshe started to get upset and cry, causing Ami to back away quickly. So when Hyki came over to poke Meowshe's ears, Meowshe smiled with joy.

"Hey!?" Ami shouted.

"For some reason, Meowshe doesn't like to be touched by anyone else…" Hyki implied in a cute voice rubbing Meowshe's head, making Meowshe's face blush, and smile harder.

Kiki stared at them and started to pout her head and eyes away, then she suddenly arose, eyes wide open.

"Kiki!" Hyki shouted.

"Huh?" Kiki responded in a shy voice.

"We need your help, come on!"

"Oh… ok!" Kiki blurted out loud in a much more happy voice.

Meanwhile

Treeoshe decided to head out to the nearby beach, ya' know, relaxation. Usually they don't do work, but then again, Treeoshe tends to put her mind to work while Penn goes off hovering over girls, still determined he does his part. Treeoshe decides to get into something Penn would like. When she came out, she sat down, and Penn sat down too drooling over her. Treeoshe suddenly turn her head towards Penn, and Penn's face suddenly paused, frowned, and put his head down as he got more serious towards Treeoshe.

"Do you think this will end all this fighting?" Treeoshe said with a cry in her voice.

"Dunno… but if it ever comes then will be ready!" Penn yelped with confidence.

In riddled with joy, she grabbed Penn with passion as he held back, and then sat back down and looked up "I'm ready too…"

Afterwards

Nevaeh hasn't been known for much, and rather keep her powers secret from everyone else. If she can show everyone what type of potential she can produce, then she will be a difficult match for everyone, and she won't be easily fooled. After a certain point, Ninga Fu took action, and kidnapped her as a hostage. While inside an unknown realm that is unreal for reality…

"What ever you are going to do to me Ninga Fu? You're going to regret it, because Hyki's going to kick your narrow behind for sure!" At this point, Nevaeh has no choice, but to utilize the power, in which she was gifted with… again.

Hyki's Amazing Pole In Ami's Hands

Meanwhile

"I need something from you Hyki…" Ami asked slowly.

"What?" Hyki pondered.

"What do you mean by 'what,' isn't going to work, anyway I need you to make a c-

Interrupted, Hyki's walkie-talkie rang. Hyki homed in on the device as Ami, Meowshe, and Kiki put their ears nearby.

"Hey, it's Treeoshe. Hyki, did you find Ami?"

"Yep… she's right here with Kiki and Meowshe"

"Sure am!" Ami said loudly.

"Well…nghah…as you can hear…nghah…something's wrong."

"A battle huh… wait you sure you can handle it out there!?"

"…Yeah, you remember telling me…nghah…earlier what the 'Maitonser Code' was at my place?"

"……What Ami and I faced before?"

"Yep, and just like you described them…nghah… they're everywhere. One day we're relaxing at the beach…nghah…next thing you know tons of them pour out walking onto shore from this…nghah… huge ship…and this huge thing, like a bunch of planets…nghah…ran through the clouds. Plus I didn't hear from Philip when I rung him…nghah…"

As Hyki's face got more serious, he went with his instincts, "Kay… I want you to take a picture of it all, with the camera I gave you!"

"What…?! What in the world would that do?!"

"Do it!"

"Fine then… I hope you know what you're doing…"

41

Hyki closed the walkie-talkie, as he turned towards the others.

"We're going to find Ninga Fu guys" Hyki said proudly.

Tugging at Hyki's shoulders, spoke, "Well… w-where do we look first Hyki?" Kiki exclaimed forward-like.

"Ha! Space my friend; the one place I love to see myself!" Hyki blurted heavily with anguish and a funny face; pointing to the sky.

"Leave?" Meowshe said with a type of fear, "B-But Meowshe doesn't w-want to leave…"

"I'll stay with Meowshe… you guys go on." Kiki said firmly.

"Great, then we're off! Ami, ready for another adventure?" Hyki said.

"Oh yeah!" Ami shouted, grinning.

Hyki bent down, and pressed a button on his side. His back pack transformed into a seat for Ami, thus she fastened in. They were about to take off when Meowshe stopped them.

"Wait!" Meowshe screamed, "Promise you'll come, p-promise Meowshe you'll come back!"

"Meowshe," Hyki said still staring into the clouds above, "I've been through a lot: making friends, new adventures, understanding obstacles… but I'll always come back to say good-bye before I leave again…"Hyki said slowly.

"…But what does that mea-

BBUURRROOOOOSSHHH! Hyki had already left, pounding into the sky. Still as they flew, they put on their radios and helmet.

"She's got a crush on you…"

"Huh, she does?"

"Of course ya fool!"

"Since when did you have a boyfriend?" Hyki said softly.

"HEY!" Ami yelped.

"Where are we going again?" Ami said comfortably, as she pretended the seat was a car.

"Somewhere where the source is good to earth, space, and Plus I can see it now. Ninga fu plans to get rid of all inhabitance on earth for some stupid reason, to destroy the earth! We've been at it for years, but this time we're gonna stop him in his tracks!" Hyki yelled heavily.

Ami looked puzzled at him but smiled brightly afterwards, "Well, let's give him all it eh!?"

"Yeah…" Hyki responded happily.

Hard to tell what it is, but they arrived at the place. Hyki used the Maitonser Code to get in by using a strand of his and Ami's hair. They walked through the place, as it t'was dark, to only use flash lights as a source of light until the lights came on. Ami was tightly squeezing Hyki's hand close by, as he blushed uncontrollably. A noise was heard and Hyki swapped out his pole and pointed it forward.

BAM! Suddenly, a hugged winged, horned robot black thing swarmed in, making Ami yell as big as the thing's mouth. Turning around quickly, eyes wide open, in shock both stood there, but there you go. Ami takes Hyki's pole out of his hand and pounces on top of the thing's head, and beats the living daylights out of the thing. Stunned watches Ami tear the thing to shreds, as he watches a-gape. Ami was getting out of control, and remembered the book of thoughts, and tried to remember something.

"AHA!" Hyki shouted, "Ami! I stole five bucks from ye wallet!"

"Wha-?" Ami said popping back to normal; fell into the scrap metal. Hyki pulled her back out into his arms, while her arms scrambled everywhere.

"Can we go home Hyki?" Ami said softly.

"Yes we can… you've done well Ami. " Hyki said disregarding the whole situation.

When they left, the place just blew up… they didn't care, but they headed off anyway.

"Can we go somewhere?" Ami asked.

"Yes, how about a picnic?" Hyki said with a smile.

"Yeah all right!"

They descended to earth as Hyki used his pole to form an electricity shield to somewhat block from the intense heat. When descending, Hyki went from running fast to slow, transforming his back-pack back again.

"Where are they?" Hyki said puzzled.

"Probably got tiered, it's the afternoon…" Ami said, continuing to run weird speeds, while something seemed to follow her, "nothing like a good run…"

On the other hand, Hyki found an old book on ducks in the trunk of the tree, with lights that bristle on it lightly. He picked it up and read it, as Ami came over to see what it is.

"What's that Hyki?" Ami asked unaware of it as she sat down next to Hyki.

Thus as the next page was turned, both saw a weird picture of ducks kissing. Alarmed, slammed their hands down on the picture simultaneously. Both looking up without a clue blushed uncontrollably, staring, as the sunset puckered in with the mountains, sank.

"Hey, it's me Ami of team 001, yeah… well after we, had our 'moment,' we settled in for the night. I slept next to Hyki real close when he told me not to, hehehe. Anyway, the next day, we woke and packed up everything, still something was wrong… we both felt it in the distance…"

Ikunashe, Kanaoshe, And Proton-Probe's Story

Thus the sun rose again, but this time brighter than yesterday's sunlight. Both Ami and Hyki woke up from a deep slumber. Hyki opened his eyes to see Ami right beside him sleep.

"...Huh, Ami!" Hyki yelled with unknown feelings.

"What? What? What!?" Ami said surprised.

"Get away from me!" Hyki said heavily.

"Woops, thought you wouldn't find out, if I was gonna wake up early, hehehe!" Ami spoke aloud calmly while she got up quickly to look at Hyki with a happy face and blush.

"Ami sometimes I don-... where is Meowshe and Kiki?" Hyki said this time with a worry. Suddenly, something popped into his brain and had an idea when he spoke.

"Uhh... Ami... could you uhh stay here until I get back. I have to pick up some things... I'll be back, oh and look out for the others if you see them!" Hyki said running off, then boosting off in the air before Ami could have a response. Ami stared at him from a distance flying away. A tear came down her cheek, but she didn't dare wipe it away.

"Happiness, when I'm with you...Hyki..." Ami said very softly to herself.

Once Ami was out of sight to Hyki, he shot straight down to the grassy surface. Thus after landing, Hyki threw open his back pack, and looked at what he had inside.

"She's gonna love it." Hyki said with happiness as he got back up and took off. When Hyki came back, he had a feeling of what Ami was eventually going to say.

"Hey Hyki...!" Ami said loudly.

"A-Wait, don't tell me!" Hyki said very loudly, "What took you so long?" Hyki said mimicking Ami and having a face of some type of chomper thing. Thus at that, Ami's face took on a gorilla face, while she folded her arms, still afterwards, they both burst into laughter.

BAM! Suddenly Ami was instantly swarmed on by huge claws by an average sized ship that flew off so fast Hyki wouldn't be able to keep up. Ami hung by its claws and stared at Hyki getting smaller and smaller as they both yelled. Their voices vanished for each. Ami looked up to see how long the arm was. So she took one finger that seemed to glow somewhat cloudy-like, and slashed it across the arm's wrist. Still before she going to drop off Ami wanted to make sure it wouldn't come back. The more they flew the more it came to be like a desert. Ami unclenched herself and slammed onto the remaining thin arm as she ran up the arm. She flushed her finger strait across the ship, while being able to land in a nearby mound of sand. The ship started to crash as it exploded, while Ami watched. Ami held her arm, because she scraped her own arm when jumping off. Ami started to look beyond that to see something big. It was some kind of huge ramp thing that was taller than she could ever think of.

The wind blew clouds of sand as though it went from light, to clouded dark. Ami walked towards the frond door on the platform, but before Ami could reach it someone came out.

"Hey what are you doing out here? You'll get lost if you don't come inside…" Said the very tall girl.

"I was just attacked by this weird ship thing!" Ami responded.

"Oh, extra parts for us… bringing them out here?" the tall girl said curiously with a smile, but Ami couldn't see herself.

"No no, an enemy attacked me…" Ami said.

"Oh, well what's your name?"

"It's Ami…"

"Do you remember me?" Ami said with a funny ponder in her voice.

"… No, but if I did it would be hard to forget you…"

"…Aren't you American… well Ami, my name's Kanaoshe… hu?… let's fix up that scratch shall we?" Kanaoshe said inviting Ami, out of the clouded sand, and into a huge room of luxury and lot's of machinery. Still when they came into the light Ami saw the girl. She was not only tall like a giant man should be: but she had long spiky black hair pointed down, peachy-brown skin, a large mechanical arm that had huge spikes for fingers as her left arm, oversized right arm, very dark dark red mini shirt that sort of covered her mouth, black pants, and dark dark red skate-looking shoes. What Ami found the feature to be jealous about was that Kanaoshe had bigger breasts than she did, but Ami only smiled as Kanaoshe smiled back.

"Wow! But doesn't it get lonely in here?"

Interrupted, a commanding voice bellowed throughout the room of the word 'hello'. Kanaoshe took a stand for it.

"Ikunashe we have a guest, that's all!" Kanaoshe bellowed back.

"Aww come on! You're not supposed to say my name!" Ikunashe said as she came down with flames pouring out of her arms and legs swarming down to the ground floor. She stood up proud and had features Ami thought might be a little scary: Her hair stood up super tall with a fire-like fade that seemed to be presume inside no matter where she turned, peachy-brown skin, very tall too, eyes burning red, shark's teeth, a long black shirt cape that covered from her mouth to her feet, black pants, and red shoes. Still what Ami found the feature to be jealous about again, was that Ikunashe had bigger breasts than she did too.

"I need a favor from you guys..." Ami said with a pout.

"We'll worry about our problems later, kay... now let's get you to Hocu, she knows all that medicine stuff." Kanaoshe said as she grabbed Ami along. The two walked along side each other as it took time to get there.

"Curious, but... uh..." Ami said stumbling in her words.

"Your wondering why my sister and I are like that... the way we're like this..." Kanaoshe said calmly not turning her head, still walking.

"You guys are sisters?!" Ami said in shock.

"...Yes... we did everything we could to get our family back, but we knew they were dead. Ikunashe and I have tried everything, but this time we decide to put our knowledge to making an android brother. We even made some for others, but our knowledge finally caught up with us causing people to chase us out of the city and into this sandy wasteland with only a few spare parts on our hands." Kanaoshe said as Ami tried to keep up with her, "So far we've got this, but we need to finish..."

"Well... I know a boy who helped me with my problems-

"No boy can help us!" Kanaoshe said quickly and angry-like.

"But it doesn't hurt to give it a try..." Ami responded softly and encouragement in her voice. Kanaoshe looked puzzled in a happy way, but before she could respond, they had already reached the nursery.

When they walked in all you could see was toys and band-aids allure, still it made Ami feel comfortable. The room had an orange glow to it. There sat 2 people. One was a girl: she had a orange cape that was wrapped around her waist, wooden blocks for shoes, orange pants, Mini t-shirt that slightly covered her mouth, weird looking orange cloths that covered her arms, peach skin, indescribable eyes, long brown flowing hair that could got down to her feet with funny looking hair spikes in front of her eyes. The other was some type of android: he had short blonde-like brown hair, peachy brown skin, no mouth but speakers on the side of his face, black sunglasses, red 'Run Away' t-shirt, black pants, and brown skate-like shoes.

"Hocu, can you patch up my friend Ami here so I can get some fresh clothes?" Kanaoshe asked.

"Sure…" Hocu said very flat.

Kanaoshe left the room as Ami sat down next to Hocu. Hocu started to get many tools, but it was very quick for her to bandage Ami up, and by then she was done. Ami saw an image on the wall; it was a frame of many people, with her and the others.

"That was quick, but what's that picture on the wall?" Ami asked with curiosity.

"…"

"Sorry I didn't know…"

"No it's alright… it's just that… I want things to be normal, like they were," Hocu presumed on, "those people, not only do I want back, but……I want us to all be friends again!" Hocu started to cry afterwards.

"I……well, doesn't your friend their get lonely too?" Ami suggested trying to cheer Hocu up.

"Oh, Proton-Probe…?" Hocu said wiping away her tears, "Proton-Probe has endured a lot without his other Probe girlfriend. I bet you he can still remember everything that happened with him and her. They showed emotion like us humans do, but she's half robot. So as of today, he hangs with his creator, Kanaoshe and others, as he searches for her, but he doesn't know if she is even alive anymore. He still gets encouraged by this photo, so he came still looking…"

"That doesn't sound good, is he upset?" Ami said.

"You're gonna have to figure it out on your own, Kanaoshe and Ikunashe have been trying at it for some time now." Hocu said getting up and out towards the room door.

"Wait… why did you decide to stay!?" Ami shouted before Hocu could leave.

"Because Ami, I found what I was looking for… I'm not afraid anymore." Hocu said as she left the room. Soon after Kanaoshe came in with fresh clothes, Ami could have, so she quickly gave them to her and left the room as she told Ami to get dressed.

Ami thought of getting dressed. They told Ami to watch Proton while they go fix up some things alone. Ami was surprised that Ikunashe and Kanaoshe left so suddenly. So Ami told Proton to sit on the bed in the room and to turn around while she got dressed. She thought since he's a robot it won't matter if she got dressed in front of him. He sat there so quietly, but she noticed that he kept turning around to stare at her belly, so she took the advantage.

"Why do you keep staring at my belly, huh?" Ami said curiously.

A pause and then, "Because I've never felt or seen anything so soft before. I'm always around machinery, and Iku and Kana never let met give them a human hug, they say it's unnecessary embracement of the body…still Kana let's me sometimes but rarely" Proton said through his speakers.

"Really?" Ami said with a side of blush on her face while thinking in her head 'this robot is just like a child,' "You know… touch my belly, come on, and don't be shy now, you can touch me if you want, eh."

So another pause and Ami sat beside him on the bed. His blush sensors went off, another pause. Suddenly he wrapped his arms around Ami's waist and somewhat made a purring sound. Ami thought, "Did he 'really,' ever had a first love before or… am I his first?" But right then something happened, a dark flare that even Ami could see rose off of him so he ran out the door. Ami was confused at first, but she continued getting dressed. Thus being done she stood up with pride in her new outfit stormed out to find the others. When Ami finally found the others she was out of breath.

"Oh Ami, we were gonna come get you…" Kanaoshe said with a smile as all 4 turned.

"Kinda too late for that huh…" Ami said painting catching her breath.

Proton-Probe handed Ami a backpack full of many advanced things as Ami thanked them.

"Well you guys… it's been great, but I gotta go find my friends now…" Ami said leaving the building but was stopped.

"Wait…!" Ikunashe said with nervousness in her voice.

"What, Ikunashe?" Ami said.

"I uhh… could you intro me on Zuman for me…" Ikunashe said even more nervously, "…cause you know gotta make friends ya know… uh you know him right?" Ikunashe said afterwards trying not to act indulged as she blushed at the same time.

"Yes, and sure…" Ami said knowing what she meant.

"Oh, and Ami… one more thing!" Kanaoshe said with a smile as Ami turned around, "I'd like to meet your friend, things might change…"

"…And one more thing for you guys," Ami said grabbing out a camera, "Hyki wanted me to do this for people who don't remember us…"

"So Hyki's his name huh?" Kanaoshe said walking towards the group.

Ami held the camera facing her and the others as they all said 'cheese'. Ami rushed out the huge building outside back to the sandy winds; she had a smile on her face and rushed forward. BAM! Suddenly Ami was snatched up by an even bigger claw by an even bigger ship that flew miles into the sky to somewhere she can't keep track of.

"Kanaoshe Moki of Team 002 is talking for *Ikunashe Moki* and *Proton-Probe.* I thought about the things Ami told me and took it to advantage, but I'd like to head back to Hyki and see what he did after Ami was taken. Anyways, a full life is sometimes…" (All Simultaneously) "… Thought between a photo!"

The Black Storm

Ami hung by its claws and Hyki stared at Ami get smaller and smaller as they both yelled, their voices vanished for each. Hyki couldn't stand of the thought of losing Ami again, no more cries. Hyki started to run off but was slowed down when a boy called his name. Hyki had seen what he looked like then stopped when he saw: he had somewhat small yellow eyes, big eyes brows, oversized black spiky hair, a black cloak with strange designs, black pants with white stripes, white shoes that seemed to be like skates in a way, and iron claws that struck around his fingers, knowing that he knew this boy. Hyki started to take off running again knowing that he couldn't see the ship in sight, but the boy said quickly out loud making Hyki stop in his tracks.

"Are you after Ninga-Fu too kid?" the boy asked loudly.

Hyki looked down then looked up and turned around with a pause.

"…Yes," Hyki said slowly.

"Then take this to defeat him," the boy said handing Hyki a simple card, like a photo, but soon after the boy started to walk away.

Suddenly the card started to flicker as blue pedals started to flip around it. Then right afterwards it slammed to the ground and then under Hyki's feet and causing it to grow up and take hold of his feet, making Hyki unable to move at the same time! Hyki gave the boy an evil look as he spoke and tried to move.

"Ngh I know who you are… ngha… your names Zuman Claw, isn't it?" Hyki said as the tangling started to look more like a rocket, "Why… ngh… why do you plan to side with Ninga-Fu!?"

"I got it from Kanaoshe… I thought it might help…" Zuman said starting to walk away as he looked back. Hyki quickly got out his picture and took his picture.

"Ha, I wonder how you're gonna turn out to be!?" Hyki said as the strangling caught up to his neck then to his face. Still a smile grew on

Zuman's face, as the expression 'huh?' came onto Hyki's face.

"Don't worry, I caught up with you guys… now go find her…" Zuman said walking away as the strangling covered Hyki's face completely. The thing turned out to be a rocket for sure, and so, it took off, fast, exiting earth.

Afterwards

Ami was suddenly thrown into a big empty room with only a table and one outlet with two men that shouted at her.

"And stay in there for all I care!" one of the men said.

When she was shoved in, her head band fell off and her long hair plopped onto the floor. Ami slowly curled into a ball pouting her head down, not uttering a sob or moving an inch, but she sat against the wall, at least trying to cry. After a point Ami looked up to notice that they didn't take her stuff away, but it was scattered across the floor. So she started to crawl towards her head band. As she picked it up, she put her hand on the table to help herself up. She thought in her mind, '*how convenient,*' as she tied her head band back on.

Meanwhile

Hyki was blasted off and the tangling ceased as it gave him more room. Buttons of all kinds Hyki seemed to recognize. All of the sudden, his walkie-talkie rang and he quickly answered it.

"Hello…?"

"*… Hyki?*"

"Huh… Ami!? Are you ok? What in the world did they do to you!?"

"*Yes I know what you're gonna say… I don't know where I am myself either… but do you know who gave you that photo?*"

"Yeah, he's the one who got me stuck in this… thing." Hyki said with a slight touch of anger.

"*His name is Zuman Claw, he's a friend of mine… he designed that rocket to help you track things down…*"

"Wait! He said that Kanaoshe gave that to him… to give to me…!"

"*No… he made that, plus he's undercover as one of the workers for Ninga-Fu!*" Ami started to shout, having the 2 people outside to say 'Quiet!'

Afterwards

"He even has his own website too…"
"Wow! How'd you learn that? "

Suddenly a screen on the ship started to appear with an innocent girls face on it.

"Hyki please help… you must face him!" The girl on the screen said as her voice and the screen started to fade.

"Face who!?" Hyki shouted as he got engaged with the conversation.

"Face…… SSCCCHHHHHSSHHH!" and then the screen went blank.

"The lines gone dead huh? Who the heck was that? Ami! Ami!" Hyki said as the connection disconnected with her too. Right afterwards, as Hyki turned around, he saw the doors on the rocket opened, and had the expression 'huh?' written on his fore head. Hyki stepped out to see a huge room that seemed endless, with mechanical objects. He saw a big device that he soon ran over to afterwards.

"A clone machine huh… but this rocket can't hold that many… unless this is a ship… COOOOOOL!" Hyki started to shout as he's closed in for the process to begin, "yeah…"

Meanwhile

After being cut offline with Hyki, Ami got enraged with such anger she almost broke the table in half when she got up, making the guards to tell her to be quiet again.

"Hyki has done enough for me… and to live it all again to see him struggle for me… no, more I'm gonna show him I wanna be their for him too!!!" Ami said enraged with anger slamming her way out the metal door to just pummel all the guards in her way, but at the same time they all looked like Zuman. BAM! Suddenly the ground shook for Ami and Hyki as the circles like before move further it evaporated into space star dust. In twirling winds went both Ami and Hyki, going far away into light only to end up being thrown out of a ship onto a small planet. A row of planets seemed to continue for a long time. Both Ami and Hyki got up feeling dizzy.

"How are we breathing!?" Hyki said noticing that they were in space.

"Where are we…?" Ami said rubbing her head.

"Some... planet... huh?" Hyki said as both Hyki and Ami looked up to see a swarm of monsters, creatures, and machines of all kinds. What Hyki saw the most revealing was that that big black thing was back and it was bigger as its eyes glistened big. Plus at the very top at some type of temple was a man, but not any man... Ninga-Fu was that man that sat afar, with a black cloak with only his eyes being able to see. He only uttered one word when they showed up.

"Begin..." Ninga-Fu said having the swarm of monsters, creatures, and machines pour at them with the black thing up front. Hyki quickly reacted to this by reaching for his pole, but something happened with Ninga-Fu's eyes that made Hyki's pole fly out of his grip. As for Ami, when she tried to flare up her finger the same thing happened to her, only that the flame went out.

"What the...he made my pole fly, and Ami Ami's flare go out!?" Hyki said during the charge. But something happened soon as Ninga-Fu said "Stop!" all the things that were coming after them stopped in place, to only hear Ninga-Fu speak his plans.

"Since you not going to last long let me let you in on a secret," Ninga Fu said as Ami and Hyki gave him a sour look, while a hologram grid popped up. "I have started this league of machines of all types to prey on the innocent. I am Ninga-Fu and I've come to make a new world, but you two are in the way... still I'll let just one of my machines get you first!" Ninga-Fu shouted as one large robot spewed a laser at both Hyki and Ami, making them scream at the top of their lungs falling to the floor. Ninga-Fu had a grin, but it soon grew to a frown when Hyki and Ami struggled back onto their feet. Still, something was wrong with Hyki; something grew that made him get up even faster than Ami. Hyki's face grew angry, and his eyes bloodshot black. A foreboding came plunging out of Ami's eyes, as a grin grew on Hyki's. Ami soon burst into tears in fear.

Hyki instantly got a flash back, not even able to remember it

"Can't you feel your Destiny arising from the depths of your own poverty and Darkness of mind? You and me... their was no relationship between us... nor love."

He came back, feeling more upset

AAAAGGGGGHHHHHHHHHH!!! Hyki screamed going full force at the machines, then the creatures, and then the monsters, as Ami tried to follow. Hyki's anger soon turned back to normal as himself too. Ami ran over to Hyki, embracing him. Into tears, to the floor, as Hyki stood straight, trying not to cry himself.

"Making Ami cry isn't going to solve anything for you Ninga-Fu…" Hyki said in his head.

"Bravo! Bravo!" Ninga-Fu said coming off the temple and onto the ground remaining calm as though nothing happened, "Why don't you let that consume you… oh and I almost forgot… I hope you like your planet crispy…"

He pointed at the grid; an asteroid was coming towards earth at an alarming speed.

The Last Shadow's Down

"You can't do that, ya deranged man!" Hyki shouted back at Ninga-Fu.

"Yes I can, look at the grid, or better yet, look afar…" Ninga-Fu said pointing out into space. Hyki looked out towards where Ninga-Fu was pointing, and there stood earth.

BBBOOOOOOOOOOOOOOOOMMMMMMMMMMMM!

The waves went pouring out everywhere, earth was gone. One thing flew back, and it landed right by Hyki as he went to pick it up. He cried softly and in his head he said 'No!' Ami cried as well. Suddenly Ninga-Fu pointed out his arm, out which dark winds seem to pull in, but it soon turned into a white glove, a fist, and so did his other arm. Ninga-Fu came rushing at both Ami and Hyki swarming attacks.

BING! BAM! SWOOSH! THUMP! DING! Attacks from Ninga-Fu came, but eventually Ami was shoved out of the way, trying to get back up. Soon it came to Hyki too, every 2 dodges Hyki gets, and Ninga-Fu gets him the third.

"Yes!" Ninga-Fu said as he continued to pummel Hyki, "Yes! Yes! Look at you, your nothing like I remembered you as… HAHA! Without your upgrade you're not even close to being a match for me! What you humans have called it earth… we call a plant!" Ninga-Fu said knocking Hyki down flat on his face. His shadow casts over Hyki, as his eyes drew black

"This is it… Time for you to- Huh?" Ninga-Fu's eyes returned to normal in shock. Hyki struggled himself up.

"Hyki?" Ami said in shock.

Hyki charged him self at Ninga-Fu, "That's not true!" Hyki said as he started to get Ninga-Fu out of his game, "All my life I wanted to help people other than myself! But you, you're nothing to me! You rather ruin others cause yours sucked! It doesn't take an upgrade to be stronger! I now understand how this upgrade was better… Cause

I have friends!!!" Hyki scorched into the air as he knocked Ninga-Fu back onto the ground, while Ami cried with happiness. Hyki quickly took his pole out and pointed it up, and got tons of electricity flowing, but it was brighter. It got brighter and brighter, but before it could finish Hyki took out the photo that was given by Zuman and threw it at Ninga-Fu.

Through Hyki's and Ami's life, they grew apart of each other and friendship and love grew as well. As it grew brighter, Ami just utterly spoke aloud.

"I will never lose when I'm with you Hyki, because... oh, you know why you big dope!" Ami said while trebling inside, but appearing strong on the outside, struggling too, "Ami, your acting strange, what's wrong?" Ami said imitating Hyki, "What's wrong with me, I'll tell you what's wrong with me! I've been holding it in for too long!... I freakin' love you gosh darnet!" A speechless spark of desire sprung the air, as the light grew it's brightest.

Everyone practically closed their eyes because it was so bright. When the light seized only the photo was left on the ground. Ami thought that even Hyki couldn't do that on his own.

"The planet isn't gone Ninga-Fu, it's too bright................." Ami heard from afar. Right afterwards Ami burst into tears, loud yelling that could be heard miles off.

"We did it together Hyki... B-b-but why did you have to go!?" Ami said holding onto Hyki's shoulder. Still before she could say anything else she turned around to see hundreds.

"Oh and not with out us too!" one of the Hyki clones said.

"You just needed to see more of what was really in you, not what you can do..." said another.

Ami couldn't say anything with tears stained on her cheek with only more to come. So she started walking towards where they last saw Ninga-Fu, holding Hyki in her arms. Suddenly the photo started to float in the air, and then it transformed into some type of hologram projector. A hologram popped up of Zuman.

"Do you gu... do you remember me?" Zuman said in complete shock. Ami was blank to answer, but just looked at Zuman.

"Uhh… leave Hyki with the clones; they'll take care of him. Come home it's urgent……" Zuman said with a worried face as he watched Ami walk slowly away taking Hyki's backpack, and then taking off.

Ami finally got back down to see the sunset, and to have a depressed face, sadden.

Ami had a flash back that made her stop in her tracks

"Those were the best of times with the team."

She returned to normal right after depressed

BAM! Out of the bushes came everyone "Surprise!!!" said everyone down to Philip, Shing, Meowshe, Penn, Treeoshe, Kiki, Kanaoshe, Ikunashe, and Zuman holding a huge cake with both Hyki and Ami's name on it.

Ami's eyes opened in shock, but soon fell to sadness and she burst into tears again as falling to the ground to have Penn catch her. Leaving the cake behind, every one came over to Ami. They all embraced each other. Suddenly something appeared out of the sunset, limping at a state, and walked towards the group as they gazed in silence.

"What no cake for me? I got a camera with one photo left…" the shadow said starting to become clear to every one.

Ami sprung up with a huge smile and a bountiful of tears ran towards the shadow to embrace it.

"Ah… HYKI!"

"*Hyki Momoshe* of team 001…… Throughout all our problems the photos are never forgotten… and some of them tuned out blank but the shedding can't proceed, because a full life is sometimes…" (Everyone Simultaneously) "… Thought between a photo!!!"